Pearl's Place

Pearl's

For Carolyn

First published in Australia 1983 by Lothian Publishing Company Pty Ltd
First published in Great Britain 1983 by Blackie & Son Ltd
First published in Picture Lions 1985
by William Collins Sons & Co Ltd
8 Grafton Street, London W1

Printed in Great Britain
by William Collins Sons & Co Ltd, Glasgow

Place

Bob Graham

FONTANA
PICTURE LIONS

Arthur lived in a big block of flats
with his Mum. He had lived there
for as long as he could remember.
His Mum worked every day and
Arthur went to school.
Sometimes he was very lonely.

The owner of the flats would
not let him have a cat or a dog
(or even a bird).
He couldn't stick his pictures
on the walls because the
sticky tape would leave marks.
Arthur managed to stick some
pictures onto the fridge with
magnets shaped like chocolates.

The doors in the corridor
had frosty glass windows.
Arthur couldn't see the
people inside but he knew
they were there.
He could hear their radios.

Sometimes he played with Anna from flat 60. Their rubber shoes squeaked on the lino in the hallway and their yells echoed down the stairwell.
The neighbours complained.

On other days, Anna and
Arthur played in the park
outside the flats.
The building blocked out the
sunlight early in the afternoon.
Swirling updraughts blew
around the building.
Newspapers and seagulls
hovered in the wind.

On Saturdays Arthur helped with
the shopping, and that's where
he and his Mum met Pearl.
She had accidentally knocked
Arthur through a stack of dog
food with her very large hip.
And just to make up, she had
insisted on giving Arthur a
wild ride in her shopping trolley.
"Just call me Pearl," she said.

Pearl was certainly very large.
She wore a bright dress like a
tent. She had tight little curls
which framed her face,
and she laughed a lot.
Arthur guessed she weighed
about two tonnes.

Pearl had a little girl called Jessica.
She wore very thick glasses
right on the end of her nose.
The glasses were smeared with
chocolate, and she constantly
poked them back with a
chocolatey finger.

"Come back to our placc
and play with Jessica,"
said Pearl.
"No thanks, got some things
to do."
Arthur looked at Jessica
with chocolate stuck in
her hair.

“We’ve got three dogs, two cats,
three hundred budgies, and
you can throw water bombs
off the roof,” Pearl said, and
put a large packet of chocolate
biscuits into her trolley.

Arthur looked at his Mum.
She nodded and his face lit up.
"Not three hundred *surely*,"
he said.

Pearl's house was old and
rambling. It was covered
in trees and flowers. The
dogs barked inside.
"Wait till you see the front
room," Pearl said as she opened
the gate for Arthur's Mum.

Arthur could see his block
of flats, which stood like
a breadknife against the sky.
A jagged shadow cut the
corner of Pearl's garden.

Then the dogs hit them!
"That's Ben and Spot and
Angie," Jessica gasped.

"Spot has been rolling in
something nasty."
She pushed her glasses
further up her nose and
sprayed Spot with the hose.

The garden had a cement fish pond.
"That's the biggest goldfish I've
ever seen," shouted Arthur.
It flicked its tail and vanished.
"I think it lives in an old gumboot
at the bottom of the pool," said
Jessica, who was topping up
the pond with a hose.

They played with the cats, caught lizards and mucked around with the water. Arthur didn't mind Jessica so much with most of the chocolate gone.

Jessica had a complete set
of swap cards, and her posters
were stuck all over the wall.
Pearl brought them a special
plate of cakes, then showed
them through the house.

They came to the front room.
There was a noise inside
like squeaky trolley wheels,
and a windy rushing of
birds' wings.
Pearl opened the door.

The room was large and
bare and full of noise.
There were hundreds of
birds. They sat in long
rows on the picture rails
and window ledges, and
talked busily with each other.

"I keep this room specially
for them," said Pearl.
Four budgerigars landed
on her head as she spoke.
Arthur's Mum brushed some
feathers from her hair.

Pot plants with little plastic
ladders stood on the window sill.
"When I am cooking," Pearl
said, "I let some of the
budgies in here, and they
climb those ladders."
She seemed to find this
very amusing and silently
shook with laughter.

Jessica shrieked with delight
as her water bomb exploded
on Arthur's head . . . SPLOSH!

". . . and if you like, you
can both come and live
in this flat at the back.
That is if Arthur doesn't
mind a few pups. Spot
is expecting them soon."

"Thank you, Pearl, we'll think about that," said Arthur's Mum.

". . . and Pearl said I can put my pictures up, and have Anna over anytime I like."

They entered the shadow
of their building.

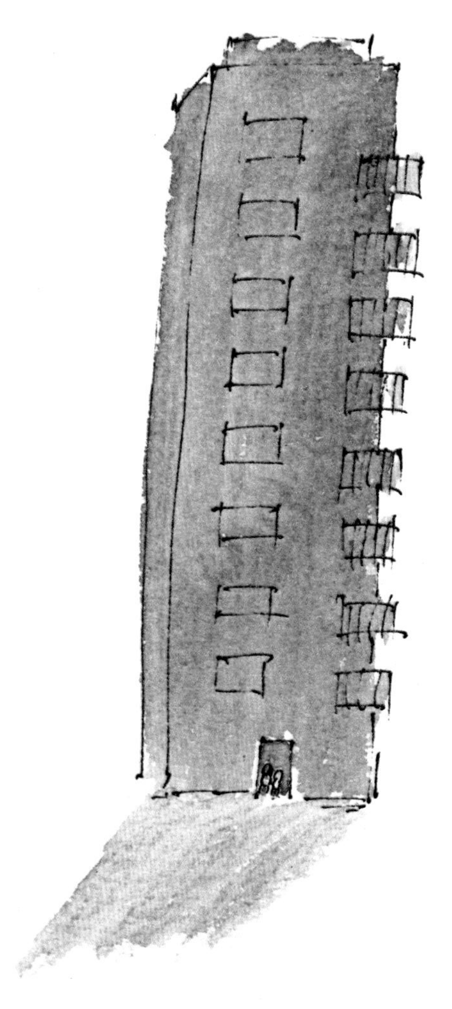

"Maybe I could take the
dogs for a walk," his
Mum said as they slowly
climbed the stairs.
Arthur smiled.